Quinito, Day and Night

Quinito, día y noche

Story / Cuento
Ina Cumpiano

Illustrations / Ilustraciones
José Ramírez

Children's Book Press • San Francisco, California

Every morning, my little sister Clara
wakes up **early**.
My big brother Juan wakes up **late**.

I don't wake up **early** or **late**.
I wake up at just the right time.
I'm Quinito. Good morning!

Por la mañana, mi hermanita Clara
se levanta **temprano**.
Mi hermano mayor Juan se levanta **tarde**.

Yo no me levanto ni **temprano** ni **tarde**.
Me levanto a la hora justa.
Yo soy Quinito. ¡Buenos días!

2

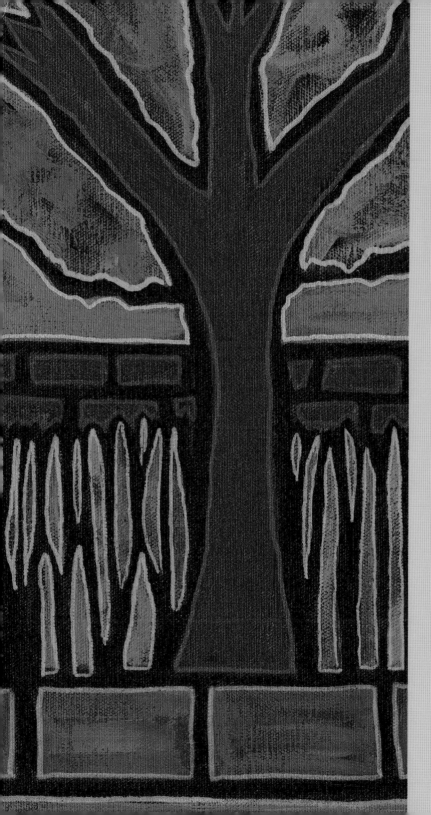

My Mami is **short**.
My Papi is **tall**.

I'm not **short**. I'm not **tall**.
I'm just the right size.

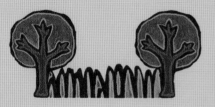

Mi mami es **baja**.
Mi papi es **alto**.

Pero yo no soy ni **bajo** ni **alto**.
Yo soy del tamaño justo.

Clara, Juan, and I are **young**.
My Grandpa Jorge and
my Grandma Inés are **old**.

Or at least, they're older than we are!

Clara, Juan y yo somos **jóvenes**.
Mi abuelito Jorge y mi abuelita Inés
son **viejos**.

O por lo menos, ¡más viejos que nosotros!

My Papi is very **neat**. He puts
everything away where it belongs.
My brother is very **messy**.
He leaves his toys everywhere.

Sometimes I'm **messy**
and sometimes I'm **neat**.
It depends on the day.

Mi papi es muy **ordenado**:
pone todo en su sitio.
Mi hermano es muy **desordenado**:
deja sus juguetes por todos lados.

Yo soy **desordenado** a veces
y, otras veces, soy **ordenado**.
Depende del día.

9

When it's **rainy**, I'm **sad**.
I can't go out to play.

When it's **sunny**, I'm **happy**.
Let's go!

Cuando **llueve**, ¡qué **triste** estoy!
No puedo ir a jugar afuera.

Cuando **hace sol**, estoy **feliz**.
¡Vámonos!

10

Juan runs **fast**.
Clara runs **slowly**, when she runs at all.

Sometimes I run **fast**,
and sometimes I run **slowly**.

Juan corre **rápido**.
Cuando Clara corre, corre **despacio**.

Yo a veces corro **rápido**, y a veces
corro **despacio**.

13

Juan climbs up, up, up.
Clara slides down, down, down.

I swing **high**. I swing **low**.
I'm the king of the swings!

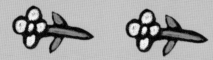

Juan **sube, sube, sube.**
Clara **baja, baja, baja.**

Me mezo **arriba**. Me mezo **abajo**.
¡Yo soy el rey del columpio!

14

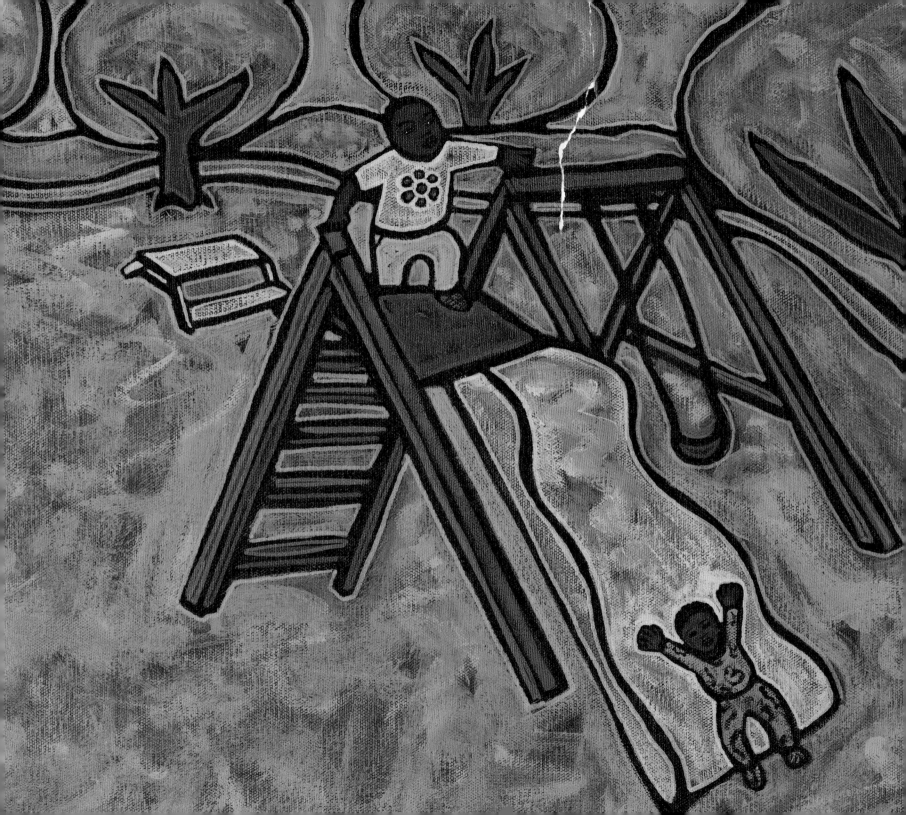

At naptime, when Clara is sleeping, we have to be very **quiet**.

But when she wakes up, we can be very **loud** . . . until Mami tells us to hush.

A la hora de la siesta, cuando duerme Clara, nos quedamos **calladitos**.

Pero cuando se despierta, somos muy **ruidosos**... hasta que Mami dice que nos callemos.

17

My parents have **long** hair.
My brother Juan and I have **short** hair.

My little sister Clara has almost
no hair at all.

Mis padres tienen el pelo **largo**.
Mi hermano Juan y yo tenemos
el pelo **corto**.

Mi hermanita Clara casi no tiene pelo.

18

That's my kitty Nieve on the **left**.
That's my puppy Carbón on the **right**.

I love to pet them before bedtime.

Ese es mi gatito Nieve a la **izquierda**.
Ese es mi perrito Carbón a la **derecha**.

A mí me encanta acariciarlos antes de acostarme.

During the **day**, I'm very busy.
At **night,** I fall asleep after Mami
sings my goodnight song.

Awake or **asleep,** I'm just me, Quinito.
Goodnight!

Durante el **día,** tengo mucho que hacer.
Por la **noche,** me duermo después que
Mami me canta una nana.

Despierto o **dormido,** yo soy yo.
Soy Quinito. ¡Buenas noches!

Ina Cumpiano is a Puerto Rican writer, the author of many little books for big kids and a few big books for little kids, among them *Quinito's Neighborhood / El vecindario de Quinito*. She edits books for teachers, plays with her eleven grandkids (big and small), writes poems (good and bad), and travels (near and far).

For Declan and Hugo in particular, and for the other nine—big and small—that I love so much. / Para Declan y para Hugo en particular, y para los otros nueve—grandes y chicos—que tanto quiero. —IC

Photo by Howard Bitterman

JOSÉ RAMÍREZ is an artist, children's book author, teacher in the Los Angeles School District, and the father of three girls: Tonantzin, Luna, and Sol. His work has been exhibited widely, and his commissions can be seen in nonprofits, hospitals, cities, film and tv companies, and cultural centers across the country.

For my daughters, Tona, Luna, and Sol, with lots of love. / Para mis hijas, Tona, Luna y Sol, con mucho cariño. —JR

Photo by Lariza Dugan-Cuadra

Publisher & Executive Director:
 Lorraine García-Nakata
Executive Editor: Dana Goldberg
Art Director: Carl Angel
Production Coordinator: Janine Macbeth
Thanks to Jadelyn Chang, Laura Chastain, Maxine Goldberg, Theresa Macbeth, Teresa Mlawer, Rosalyn Sheff, Kristl Wong, and the CBP staff: Imelda Cruz, Rod Lowe, Janet del Mundo, and Christina Troup.

For a free catalog, write: Children's Book Press, 965 Mission Street, Suite 425, San Francisco, California, 94103. Visit us on the web at: www.childrensbookpress.org

Printed in Hong Kong by Marwin Productions
10 9 8 7 6 5 4 3 2 1

Distributed to the book trade by Publishers Group West. Quantity discounts available through the publisher for nonprofit use.

Children's Book Press is a 501(c)(3) nonprofit organization. Our work is made possible in part through the generosity of the following contributors: AT&T Foundation, John Crew and Sheila Gadsden, the San Francisco Foundation, the San Francisco Arts Commission, Horizons Foundation, the National Endowment for the Arts, Union Bank of California, the Children's Book Press Board of Directors, Elizabeth Ports, and the Anonymous Fund of the Greater Houston Community Foundation.

Library of Congress Cataloging-in-Publication Data
Cumpiano, Ina.
 Quinito, day and night / story, Ina Cumpiano; illustrations, José Ramírez = Quinito, día y noche/cuento, Ina Cumpiano; ilustraciones, José Ramírez.
 p. cm.
 Summary: Little Quinito and his family take the reader through a day filled with opposites, including short/tall, quiet/loud, and rainy/sunny.
 ISBN 978-0-89239-226-1
[1. English language—Synonyms and antonyms—Fiction. 2. Family life—Fiction. 3. Hispanic Americans—Fiction. 4. Spanish language materials—Bilingual.] I. Ramírez, José, ill. II. Title. III. Title: Quinito, día y noche.
 PZ73.C85 2008
 [E]—dc22   2007050008

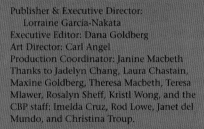

A bilingual glossary of opposites / Un glosario bilingüe de opuestos

day and night / día y noche

early and late / temprano y tarde

short and tall / bajo y alto

young and old / joven y viejo

neat and messy / ordenado y desordenado

to rain and to be sunny / llover y hacer sol

happy and sad / feliz y triste

fast and slow / rápido y despacio

high and low / arriba y abajo

to climb and to descend / subir y bajar

quiet and loud / callados y ruidosos

long and short / largo y corto

right and left / derecha e izquierda